Ever wondered what Snow W...
Seven Dwarfs would be like if:

a. Snow White was a snow monster?
b. The dwarfs were ninjas?
c. The mean old stepmother was a super hero?
d. The handsome prince was a vampire?
e. All of the above!?

ME TOO!!

Luckily for you, I've been stuck at home all school holidays with nothing to do and my annoying sister had a copy of Snow White just lying around. (OK, technically I had to sneak into her bedroom while she was at ballet camp and 'borrow' it – but I'm sure she won't mind at all!)

So here it is – the totally epic, new and improved, modern-day masterpiece...

SNOW MAN AND THE SEVEN NINJAS!

Enjoy!

buckets
ainsaws
squirted
zombies
shrieked
bigger
slingshot
super
monster
random
poison
ouch!
undies
boogers

Dedicated to my beautiful wife,
Eva-Janet

Koala Books
An imprint of
Scholastic Australia Pty Limited
PO Box 579 Gosford NSW 2250
ABN 11 000 614 577
www.scholastic.com.au

Part of the Scholastic Group
Sydney • Auckland • New York • Toronto • London • Mexico City
• New Delhi • Hong Kong • Buenos Aires • Puerto Rico

Published by Scholastic Australia in 2017

National Library of Australia Cataloguing-in-Publication entry
Creator: Cosgrove, Matt, author, illustrator.
Title: Snow man and the seven ninjas / Matt Cosgrove author and illustrator.
ISBN: 9781743811696 (paperback)
Series: Cosgrove, Matt, Epic fail tales ; no.1
Target Audience: For primary school age.
Subjects: Fairy tales. Wit and humor, Juvenile.
Dewey Number: A823.3

Typeset in Adobe Garamond, Campland Letters and Grafolita Script
by the author/illustrator ← Control freak!

Printed in Australia by Griffin Press.

Scholastic Australia's policy, in association with Griffin Press, is to use papers that are renewable and made efficiently from wood grown in responsibly managed forests, so as to minimise its environmental footprint.

17 18 19 20 21 / 1

Happy Birthday
Smelly,
I hope you don't
like the book,
love Nan xxoo
PS – I have always
loved your brother more
because he is awesome
and you smell!

APPLAUSE
Once upon a swine...
THIS ISN'T GOING TO END WELL
THIS ACT IS A BIT HAMMY!
WHAT A STAGE HOG!
IT'S REALLY A BOAR!
MMMM... BACON!

… there rode a beauty queen.

One contest day, she was sitting on her black, spotted pet pig, smiling out at the audience while juggling her boyfriend's chainsaws, blindfolded!

Accidentally, she sliced her fingers off!

Three buckets of blood squirted on the judges.

'AAAAARRRRGGGGHHHH!!!!!!

My fingers,' she screamed.

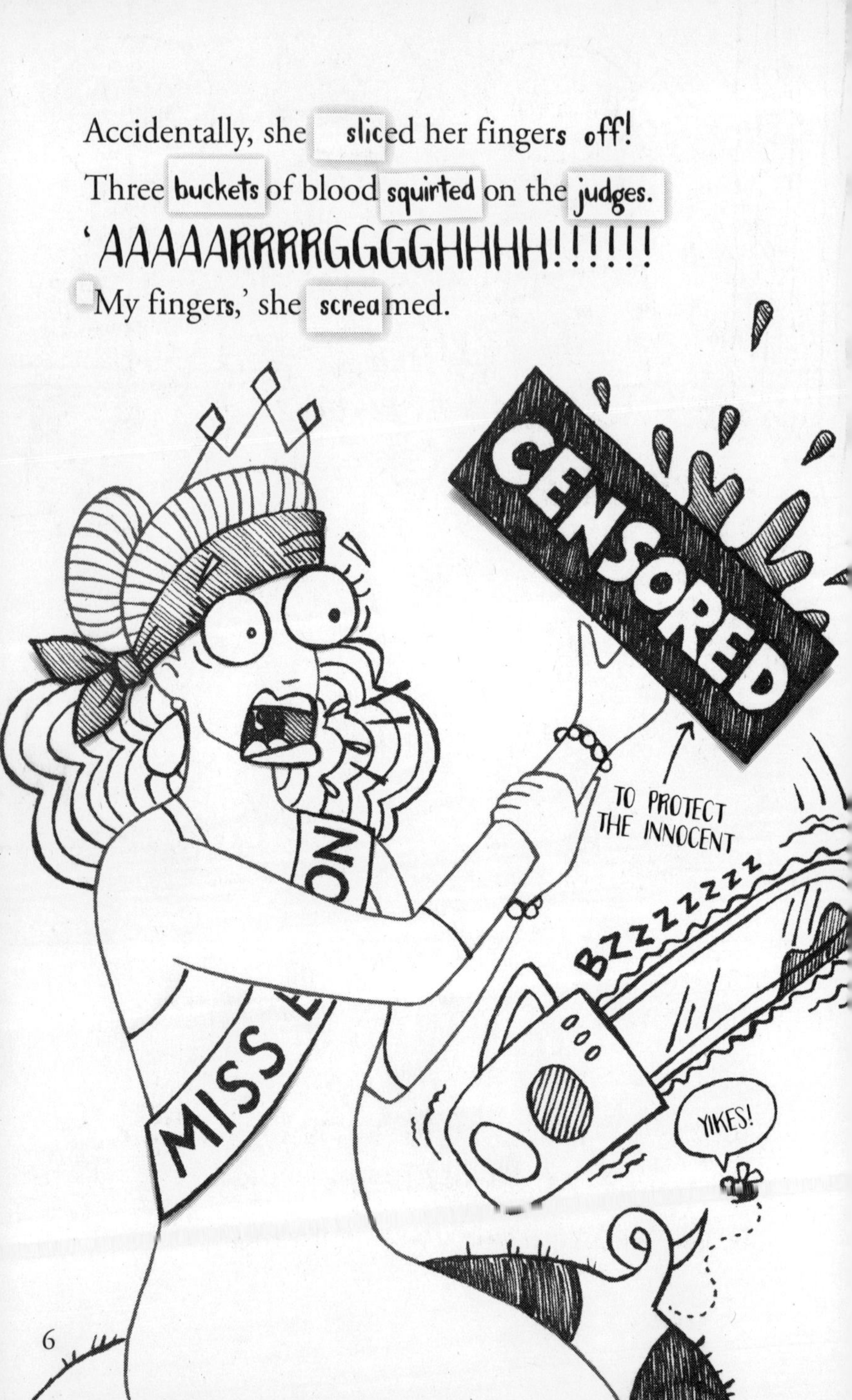

The lack of blood made her remark stupidly, 'Oh, how I wish for a monster made of snow, with eyes as red as blood and muscles as big as the butt of this pig.' And then she croaked. Worse than that, she only placed third runner-up in the talent section! How embarrassing!!

Shortly after lunch, her weird dying wish was magically granted when a little monster came onto the stage. He was indeed made of snow, with eyes as red as blood and muscles as big as a pig's butt. The judges named him Snow Man... and best new talent!

'We'll be back after only a few short ads,' the host said. The little monster made up his mind to come back next year with a brand-new act! He was hooked on the fame, on the applause, on the spotlight!

Meanwhile, on the other side of town...
this random, new super hero dude, although very muscly, was very proud and cruel... and a total fitness freak!

He hated the thought that anyone could be stronger than him. Over the years, he had collected many exercise machines (as seen on TV!) but his most beloved possession was a magic mirror/television.

Each day, he would pose in front of the mirror for hours on end, admiring his muscles and applying his fake tan. When he was finished loving himself sick, he would ask the mirror/television:

'Mirror, mirror on the wall,
Who is the fittest of them all?'

The mirror would always reply:
'You are the fittest, you're ideal,
With abs of iron, buns of steel!'

This pleased the super dude, for
he knew the mirror could not lie.

Meanwhile, on the other side of town...

Little Snow Man grew up and became bigger and hairier, and with each push-up was more muscly than before. All those who saw him marvelled at his sixpack and were certain that never before had such abdominals existed. Surely, no act could compete with the beefcake Snow Man, they thought.

HE'S SO SWEATY... YETI'S SO HANDSOME!
CHECK OUT THOSE ABS!

Meanwhile, back on the other side of town...

One morning, the super dude gazed upon his reflection in the mirror and asked his usual question:

'Mirror, mirror on the wall,
Who is the fittest of them all?'

However, this time, the answer was not what he expected.

'You may have a nice sixpack,
But you also have a hairy back!
The one with abs that make me blush,
Is the young Snow Man, you toilet brush!'

The super dude flew into a wall. It really hurt!
His undies turned inside out with envy.
(Technically known as the Kamikaze, Totally Jelly, Self-Destructing Green-Eyed Wedgie)
It really, REALLY hurt!

He vowed he would destroy Snow Man.
But how could he get rid of the monster?
Snow Man was a popular star and the wicked super dude did not dare to show his hatred for the muscly monster in public.
That would be super bad for his image.
Then he thought of a cunning plan!
The super dude called up the stunt man who worked for Snow Man, as part of his new act.

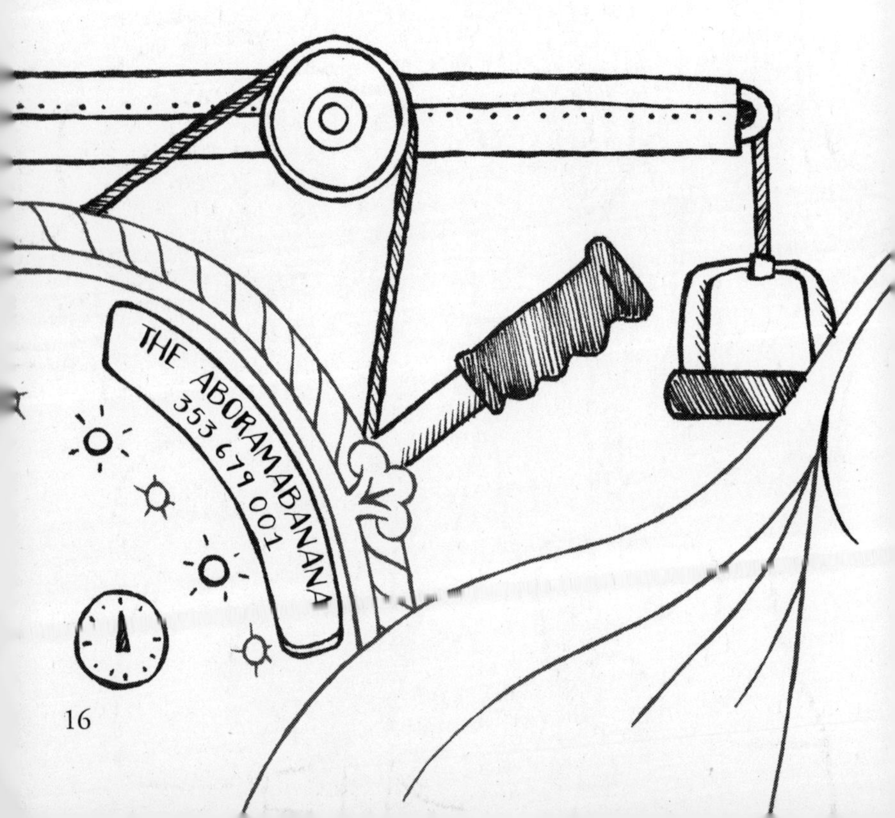

HEY, IT'S STUNT MAN! I'M OUT DOING SOMETHING DANGEROUSLY AWESOME OR AWESOMELY DANGEROUS SO PLEASE LEAVE A MESSAGE AFTER THE BEEP.
UH... I HATE LEAVING MESSAGES.
Stuntman
BEEP.
OH, HEY STUNT MAN. SUPER DUDE HERE. DON'T KNOW IF YOU REMEMBER ME? WE MET AT THAT THING. I'M A BIG FAN. ANYWAY, I WAS...
BEEP.
URGH!

Later that day, after several phone messages...
'I have a job for you,' he told the stunt man.
'You must make Snow Man into a laughing stock then slay him and bring me back some Chinese takeaway as a snack. There's fifty bucks in it for you!'

The stunt man was horrified at the super dude's command, but he was so frightened of his powers and what he might do to the stunt man's pet goldfish that he promised to do as ordered. The super dude laughed evilly.

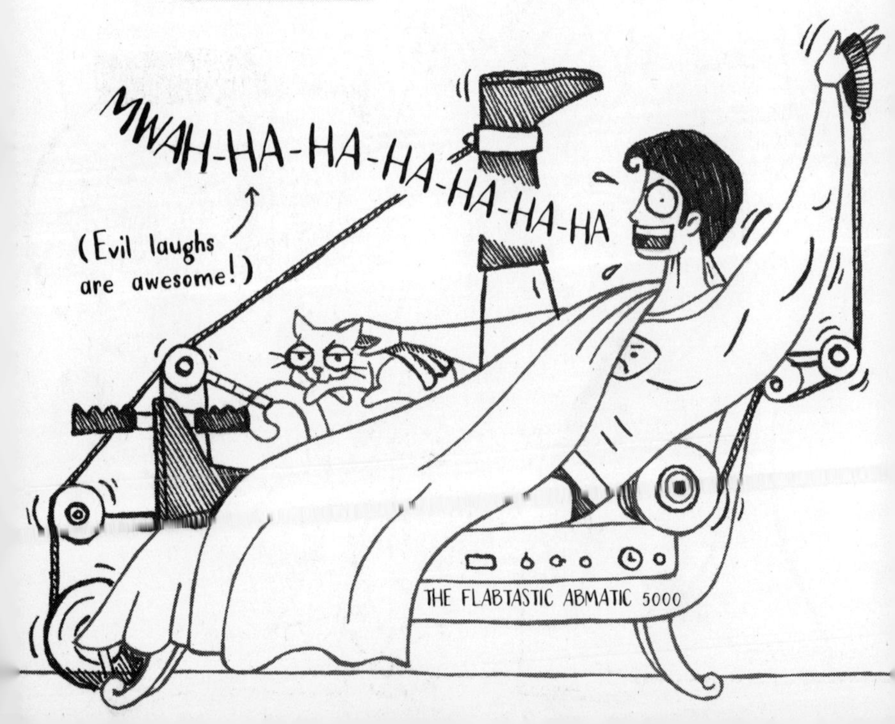

SUPER HEAT RAYS
SUPER FREEZE BREATH
SUPER SLAM DUNK
SUPER HOME RUN
SUPER CANNON BOWL
SUPER KITTY SNACK
SPLASHY! NOOOO! I LOVE YOU!!
SUPER FLUSH

The very next day the stunt man followed Snow Man onto the stage ready to perform their talent-show act. When they reached the middle of the show, he took out his throwing knife collection. The crowd gasped!

'Prepare to be annihilated Snow Man,' he hollered loudly. The crowd cheered!

THE ABDOMINAL
SNOWMAN
LIVE

The blade glistened in the spotlight as the stunt man threw the knife above the terrified monster's head. The crowd went wild!

'That was kinda close!' shrieked Snow Man. 'And I don't think that's the rubber knife from rehearsals.'

Suddenly, the stunt man took aim at him and hurled his next knife. Then another. Then another. Then another. Then another. Then another. And another.

And then the stunt man took aim at him and squirted his water pistol filled with lemon juice right into Snow Man's eyes.

And then the stunt man took aim at him and released his slingshot filled with brussels sprouts.

And then the stunt man took aim at him and fired his rocket launcher filled with zombie guinea pigs.

And then the stunt man took ping pong balls and smashed them, shot after shot, straight at Snow Man's forehead.

And then the stunt man took his finger and flicked his slimy boogers right at Snow Man.

Finally, the stunt man took out a brand-new fart gun, shooting toxic balls of stinky gas at Snow Man.

The crowd burst into fits of laughter.
Even though he had all those big muscles,
Snow Man was a total wimp!

'Stop laughing at me! Just stop it! I'm going to run away and never come back!'
The stunt man tripped him. Snow Man tumbled and dive-bombed into the audience.

HA HA
BOO!
HISS!
HA HA

The stunt man hunted down Snow Man in the crowd, shooting him with his crossbow. It was a direct hit!

The arrow pierced Snow Man's pinky finger and the monster squealed his lungs out and completely fainted, as the ~~p~~roof of the theatre collapsed, burying him.

The stunt man returned his overdue library books and presented the super dude with his takeaway which he proceeded to eat with relish and mustard and tomato sauce and gherkins and anchovy paste.

But what of Snow Man?

Deep in the rubble, all hurty and so terribly embarrassed, the poor monster punched and kicked until he finally reached the light.

'What am I to do?' he wondered.

'I can't return to the stage now, for the people shall totally laugh at me again,' he sobbed. 'But where can I go? How shall I live with the shame?'

It was then that Snow Man remembered a late-night commercial from the television.

'I shall go and ask for training,' Snow Man decided. 'Surely the seven ninjas who teach in the temple will make me the best act ever! This will be the comeback of the century!'

The door to the temple was locked, so Snow Man roughly pulled it off its hinges and threw it aside.

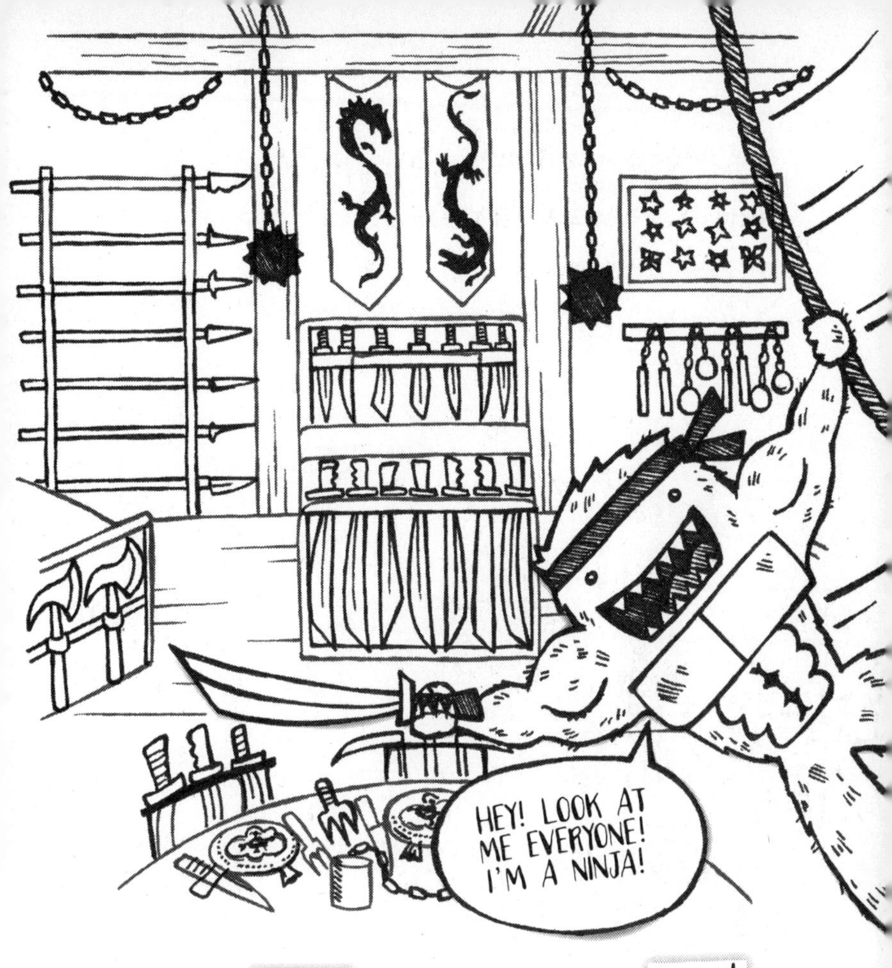

Inside the temple, everything looked so lethal! Snow Man went nuts, playing with everything! In the middle of the room was a giant weapons rack, filled with seven sharp swords and seven shiny daggers. Against the wall were seven deadly staffs, each covered with different poisoned spikes!

Being both dumb and stupid, Snow Man licked a tiny morsel of poison from each spike and took a ninja star from the display case clearly labelled "DO NOT TOUCH".

After that, a big cage fell down on him and Snow Man was soon trapped! He then passed out from the poison.

Not long afterwards, the owners of the temple, the seven ninjas, returned home from their long day of shopping at the mall.

Upon entering the temple, the first ninja, Snotty, said, 'Someone has torn the door off! My revenge will be swift and without mercy!' Then he picked a juicy booger from his nostril and popped it in his mouth.

The second ninja, Farty, said, 'Someone has been touching my Whoopee Cushions of Doom! They shall pay dearly for this insult! Whoops. Excuse me,' as he let a ripe one rip.

The third ninja, Burpy, said, 'BBBBBEEEEE-EEEEELLLLCC--CCCCHHHH!'

The fourth **ninja**, **Scabby***, said, 'Who has been eating my **secret** scab collection? I was saving that for dessert!'

* AUTHOR'S NOTE: ANY RESEMBLANCE TO MY SISTER – 'SMELLY' – IS TOTALLY ON PURPOSE!!

The fifth **ninja**, **Pukey**, said, **'Eeerrggghhhhh! You're so gross!'** and spewed all over the floor.

The sixth ninja, Phlegmy, said, 'Who has been licking all my poisoned spikes? What an absolute idiot!'

The seventh ninja, Fred, said, 'I think someone has broken into the temple!'

'Oh really?!' said Scabby.
'You think so?!' said Burpy.
'Thanks Captain Obvious!' the other ninjas yelled at him. (No-one really liked Fred.)

Imagine their surprise when they found Snow Man caught in one of their traps.

'How smelly he is,' they cried, holding their noses closed so they could escape his stench. 'Let him hang in there and we shall spray him with a high-powered hose,' they decided, as they hoisted the cage into the air.

Then the rope broke and Snow Man fell suddenly from his prison with a thud, surprised to find himself surrounded by seven ninjas, all looking really mad!

The ninjas frowned meanly at him, tying the young monster to a chair.

'Who are you, dirty thief?' Phlegmy asked, spitting saliva all over Snow Man's face.

'Why have you entered our temple, scumbag?' Farty asked, letting another juicy one rip.

'My name is Snow Man. I am the star of a talent show. I'm kind of a big deal! But in my last performance a stunt man tried to slay me. I escaped with my dignity in shreds, totally, utterly humiliated! Now I have no nerves to go back on the stage. Will you help me, wise ninjas? Give me my confidence back. Rebuild me – better, fitter, stronger – so that I am the best talent act the world has ever seen!'

The seven ninjas listened attentively.

'You can train with us now, for it is clear you may never return to the stage while you're in this condition, you pathetic bacteria, scraped from the fingernail of a bottom-scratching baboon!'

'If you promise to take orders from us, clean our toilet, eat our specially prepared meals, do our exercise plan, wash our pet skunk and any other tasks we demand, then you shall become the best performer in the galaxy, you miserable drop of pond scum squeezed from the armpit of a wart-licking toad!'

Snow Man answered, 'Yes, with all my heart and soul, I promise to take orders from you until my triumphant return to the stage!'

And so it came to be that Snow Man trained with the seven ninjas. Each morning the seven ninjas went to town on the monster. He slaved his behind off in the temple — cleaning their toilet, completing their deadly obstacle courses, rehearsing and exercising. When he finally collapsed — hungry and tired — the ninjas would have something disgusting to eat, ready as a challenge for Snow Man.

'We have made a good test for you!' said one of the ninjas. 'You must eat the hottest chilli in the kingdom, you dried-up ball of earwax from a deformed dung beetle!'

Snow Man's face lit up. Smoke came out his ears. Flames came out his nose.

It was so HOT in his mouth!

The ninjas laughed. 'You are making progress, you worthless toenail clipping from a sewer-dwelling cockroach!'

The ninjas, however, were worried he was still too soft and would once again try to exterminate him as part of his training.

They warned Snow Man to never let anyone enter the temple while they were at the games arcade, as his training required total isolation.

Meanwhile... on the other side of the town, the super dude was content, convinced he was once again the most muscly guy of all.

One day, he stepped before his mirror/television and asked:

'Mirror, mirror on the wall,
Who is the fittest of them all?'

And the mirror replied:

'You are just an old has-been,
'Cos Snow Man's still the fittest seen.
He trains with the ninjas up the road a bit,
And he's more buff than you, you silly twit!'

The super dude was furious when he heard this for he knew the mirror could not lie and that the stunt man had failed him.

SOMEBODY GET SOME ICE... 'COS YOU JUST GOT BURNED!

WHAT'S
HOT
HOT-O-METER
WHAT'S
NOT

Day and night ~~s~~he thought of how ~~s~~he might destroy Snow Man. At last a plan came to him. He disguised himself as a police woman and made his way through the city until ~~s~~he came to the temple of the seven ninjas. Then ~~s~~he banged on the door. (The ninjas had forced Snow Man to rebuild the door using only toothpicks and Phlegmy's saliva as glue.)

'Open up, slimeball! You are under arrest, pal,' the disguised super dude called to Snow Man, who was peering out through the window.

'Come out dirtbag, and put your hands up or this won't be pretty, scum bucket!'

'My ninjas do not like me speaking with anyone but I am sure they would want me to obey the law,' murmured Snow Man.

So Snow Man opened the door.

'Here are a nice big pair of boxing gloves for you,' said the police woman to Snow Man. 'Let me demonstrate what I can do with them.'

Law-abiding Snow Man let the police woman punch him up. All the breath left Snow Man's body and he fell down on the steps, lifeless. The super dude flew off into the sky thinking Snow Man was finished. 'Evil laugh time: Mwah-ha-ha-ha-ha-ha-ha-ha-ha-ha!'

Luckily the ninjas returned to the temple from their day at the games arcade early that evening. They found Snow Man collapsed on the step and slapped him around his face, then gave him a wet willy over and over again.

Little by little he began to revive and the ninjas carried him inside and dropped him down on a bed of nails.

'Who gave you the black eyes?' they asked Snow Man, and he told them about the police woman.

They guessed it was just a completely random incident and warned him to never go swimming until thirty minutes after eating.

'Now, to find out if you are still weak, we will try to do away with you again,' they said gravely, and they dropped him into a tank of hungry piranhas.

Meanwhile, on the other side of town...

As soon as the super dude was back at his secret headquarters, he rushed to his mirror/television.

'Mirror, mirror on the wall,
Who is the fittest of them all?'
And the mirror replied:
'You're fit, but you're not fit enough,
'Cos Snow Man's still the hottest stuff!
He works out with the ninjas, and is the best.
And would kick your butt in a muscle contest'

The super dude knew his plan had failed and was furious, stamping his feet on the floor and pounding the walls with his fists. Again he came up with another plan to end Snow Man.

NEXT TOP MONSTER
VOTED BY YOU:
HOTTEST GUY ALIVE!
SNOW MAN:
"I WAS BORN THIS WAY BABY!"
SNOW MAN REVEALS HIS 6 PACK SECRETS
HOTTER THAN ANY HERO
MORE MUSCLES

Using his super powers, he made a turbo-powered hair dryer. He disguised himself as a door-to-door sales lady and once again came to the ninjas' temple.

"She" knocked on the door and called out, 'I have some turbo hair dryers to sell.'

Snow Man peered from the window and saw the powerful hair dryer the sales lady held. It was awesome and he imagined how it would fluff up his hair for his comeback performance!

He forgot the motto of the ninjas: "never trust a hair dryer sales lady" and opened the door.

'Now let me show you how lovely this will fluff up your hair,' the sales lady said. As soon as the turbo-powered hair dryer blew on his filthy, icy body, the heat started to increase and Snow Man began to melt more and more.

The disguised super dude looked down at the puddle by his feet and laughed his evil laugh, before flying back into the clouds.

'Mwah-ha-ha-ha-ha-ha-ha-ha-ha-ha-ha-ha!'

Later on, the ninjas returned to find the Snow Man puddle, lying on the doorstep of their temple. They saw the turbo hair dryer still plugged in the socket and pulled it out, 'Safety first!', then scooped up the melted snow in a bucket and carried it inside.

'We are not too late,' one of the ninjas cried. 'We can still save him.'

They placed the melted snow in their freezer and when it was totally frozen they slowly carved him from the block of ice, giving him even bigger muscles than before.

When ~~s~~he was finished, Snow Man told of the door-to-door sales woman and the hair dryer. The ninjas scolded him and told him firmly, 'You must not forget the ninja motto again you foul nose hair from a flatulent warthog – "Never trust a hair dryer sales lady". How many times do we have to tell you?'

'Be prepared! For your punishment, we shall try to eliminate you again.' And they smeared him in honey and released a barrel of lethal fire ants.

Back at his headquarters the super dude had just discovered that Snow Man was still alive and screamed in fury. This time he declared he would finish Snow Man once and for all!

Realising even his most evil super powers couldn't hurt that stupid Snow Man on the outside, it looked like he would have to attack Snow Man from the inside! The start of the plan was to mess with Snow Man's fragile mind. 'That will destroy him!' Insert evil laugh: 'Mwah-ha-ha-ha-ha-ha-ha!'

Once more the super dude disguised himself — this time as a teenage fan — and set off into the city. When the super dude arrived at the temple, he knocked on the door.

'I cannot open the door,' Snow Man called from the window. 'I have promised the ninjas I will not let anybody in.'

'Please! You need to open the door. I'm your number-one fan! I have travelled a long way to see your amazing show. Surely you will perform one act for me?'

The young fan seemed so sweet, and Snow Man so missed the sound of applause, he eventually decided he should perform the show.

Snow Man opened the show, bowing down to hear the applause, then began performing what the ninjas had taught him.

'I'm not afraid, anymore!' said Snow Man joyously. 'Look at me! I shall take the world by storm!'

'Fabulous!' screamed the fan.

Snow Man said, 'Oh, it feels so good! Nothing can harm me now! I'm back, baby!'

'Then let me give you a taste of this, Snow Man!'

Suddenly, the young fan hurled rotten tomatoes up at Snow Man, who took a hit right in the face! Then Snow Man's number-one fan started to heckle.

The heckling worked immediately and Snow Man began to tremble and sweat. He clutched at his chest in panic, realising he had been a flop again and was dying on stage! With a final gasp he fell to the ground.

The evil super dude looked at the lifeless body of Snow Man and laughed his evil laugh.

'Mwah-ha-ha-ha! I repeat: Mwah-ha-ha-ha!'

'This time the ninjas will never be able to stage a comeback. You're finished Snow Man!'

He flew from the temple back to his HQ and went straight to his mirror/television.

'Mirror, mirror on the wall,
Who is the fittest of them all?'
And this time the mirror replied:
'You are the fittest, super guy,
Since Snow Man has said bye-bye.'

The super dude breathed a sigh of relief.
'At last, I am the most muscly guy in this land!'
He quickly forgot about Snow Man as he posed, admiring his muscles in the magic mirror until he fell off his stool.

Back at the temple, the seven ninjas arrived home to find Snow Man lying on the floor. There was no sign of life in his body. Snow Man was a goner.

The ninjas gathered around playing minigolf on him for three hours, until Farty said 'What should we do with the body? He's really starting to stink!'

'He is too muscly to bury in the cold, dark ground,' one of the ninjas declared.

'It will take ages to dig a hole big enough!'

'Let us place him in our old fridge. I bet everyone in the world would pay big bucks to see him now! We could make a fortune out of this!'

When this was done, the seventh ninja painted the name — Snow Man — in gold letters on a big sign, and underneath he put the words — "$20 A PHOTO".

The ninjas placed the old fridge on a large rock outside their temple. One of them always remained, collecting all the money.

For almost a year, Snow Man lay peacefully in his refrigerator, his muscles unchanged. He seemed to be even more muscly than ever, and everyone wanted to take a selfie with him. It was the number-one tourist attraction in town!

One day, a really rich vampire was travelling through the city and came upon Snow Man. He looked so peaceful lying in the refrigerator that the vampire fell in love with the idea of having this fridge as his very own bed/coffin. 'I must have it!' he said to the ninja guarding the attraction. 'Let me have this fridge. I shall pay you whatever you like for it. It will make a totally awesome coffin! I'll be so chillin' in there. I can have a snack without even getting out of bed! This is literally the coolest thing ever!'

The ninja replied, 'OK we will sell it for all the gold in the world. Kerching!'

'Sure, whatever, money's no object...
Now give me a hand,' pleaded the vampire,
'For I cannot move it with Snow Man still inside.
It's way too heavy!'

When the ninjas realised that the vampire was right, (it really was heavy), they agreed to let him turn Snow Man into a vampire, too.

Overjoyed, the vampire leant over and took a massive bite out of Snow Man's neck.

Snow Man suddenly opened his eyes and sat up in the fridge. 'Where am I?' he asked.

'You're in front of the temple in an old refrigerator and you've just been turned into a vampire. Keep up with the plot, you idiotic skid mark from the underpants of a toilet-trained orangutan!' Scabby yelled.

Too excited to speak, the vampire rushed towards him and lifted him out of the fridge. (Vampire snow monsters are way lighter than normal snow monsters.)

Then he proclaimed his love for his new coffin.

'Will you carry my fridge?' the vampire asked Snow Man. 'It's still kinda heavy and you're all big and muscly, and I have a bad back.'

'Yes!' he replied, 'But on one condition. That we shall perform together as Snow Man and vampire as it would be the best show ever! And the seven ninjas are invited to our premiere performance.'

'Um, that's two conditions. But sure! I've got all eternity. What else am I going to do to pass the time?' said the vampire.

And so the vampire and Snow Man prepared for their new show, the most spectacular act ever seen in the ~~land.~~ ~~world~~ ~~solar system~~ ~~galaxy~~ UNIVERSE! Yeah, it was THAT good!

Blood-sucking vampires! Muscle-bound snow monsters! Death-defying stunts of sheer stupidity! Catchy tunes! WHAT MORE COULD ANYONE WANT?

By chance, the super dude was also invited to the premiere. Preparing to go and dressed in his fancy pants, he posed in front of his mirror and asked:

'Mirror, mirror on the wall,
Who is the fittest of them all?'
And the mirror replied:
'You were the fittest, Super Bore,
But Snow Man's back, fitter than before!
His sixpack is an eightpack now,
And his biceps and pecs make me go, WOW!'

The super dude was furious and screamed in a rage. Wild with anger, he picked up a dumbbell and hurled it at the mirror, which shattered into a thousand pieces.

He decided he must still go to the premiere performance to see Snow Man's abs for himself.

He burst into the theatre as the show was beginning, and saw before him the muscly star — Snow Man, tap-dancing over a vat of bubbling acid while the vampire rode a unicycle and juggled angry scorpions.

He howled with disbelief and anger. 'It's not fair! I must be the most muscly!' the super dude screamed. Snow Man turned to see who had interrupted his performance.

'No-one stops my show! No-one steals my spotlight! This is my time to shine!' he muttered. 'Prepare to pay, vaguely-familiar stranger!'

All the ninja training and exercise that filled his mind, body and heart exploded out and she began to attack the super dude.

Soon there was nothing left of the super dude but a pile of minced meat.

The seven ninjas cheered that the interrupting super dude was whipped good by Snow Man! Finally their pathetic student had learned something!

The show continued and Snow Man and the vampire became the hottest act in the world – and eventually the universe! – and they performed . . .

happily ever after... until one day a giant meteorite came crashing down, destroying them all!

The squishy End

The Moral of the Story:
Don't waste your time staring in the mirror or worrying about getting a sixpack because any second a giant meteorite could come crashing down and – KABOOM – you're toast!

BRAINS!
Coming Soon in the
EPIC FAIL TALES
Series
AARRGHH!
SAVE US SUPER DUDE!
WEREN'T YOU PAYING ATTENTION? SUPER DUDE'S MINCED MEAT. PAGE 91!!

ATTACK OF THE GIANT ROBOT ZOMBIE MERMAID

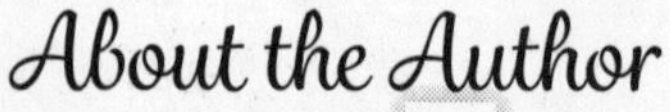

About the Author

Splatt Cosgrove is an idiot and embarrassment to his whole family, who lives in an old wheelie bin with his pet rock and two monkeys.

He spends his days wearing pink tutus and loves making kids barf with his terrible body odour!

Photo: Eva Amores